W9-BVE-130

Big Cat Dreaming

MARGARET WILD
Illustrated by Anne Spudvilas

Annick Press Ltd.
Toronto • New York

In the holidays my little sister Naomi and I stay at Grandma's. She has a big, spooky house and a big, spooky garden.

Best of all, she has Big Cat
and Small Dog.

Late one afternoon, I sit with Big Cat on my lap.
Big Cat twitches and moans in her sleep.

'Do cats dream?' asks Naomi.

'Of course,' I say. 'Cats dream of fish and meatballs.'

But Grandma says, 'I think cats dream of
when they were kittens . . .

. . . firecracker kittens, full of fizz and hiss.'

Naomi sprawls with Small Dog on her stomach.
Small Dog flicks his ears and grunts in his sleep.

'Do dogs dream?' asks Naomi.

'Of course,' I say. 'Dogs dream of bones and interesting smells.'

But Grandma says, 'I think dogs dream of when they were pups . . .

. . . cheeky-tailed pups, digging here,
digging there, chewing this, chewing that.'

Naomi and I snuggle up next to Grandma on the sofa. Her eyelids quiver and she makes whistling noises in her sleep.

'Do grandmas dream?' asks Naomi.

'Of course,' I say. 'Grandmas dream of gardening and comfy slippers and olden days music.'

When Grandma wakes up, we ask her what she dreams, and she says, 'I dream of when I was a girl . . .

. . . when after dinner
we children swarmed
out of our houses and
joined in a wild game of
hide-and-seek. We dived
behind shrubs, hid in the
deepest shadows, and we
waited, grinning in the
dark, for the shout of
"Coming! Ready or not!"'

'Lucky thing,' says Naomi. 'Our garden at home is as small as a towel. There is nowhere to run, nowhere to hide.'

'Tell you what,' says Grandma. 'Let's ask Asha and Sanjay from next door to come for dinner, and afterwards you four can play hide-and-seek. In the dark!'

'Yeah!' says Naomi, scratching Small Dog behind the ears.

'Yeah! Yeah!' I say.

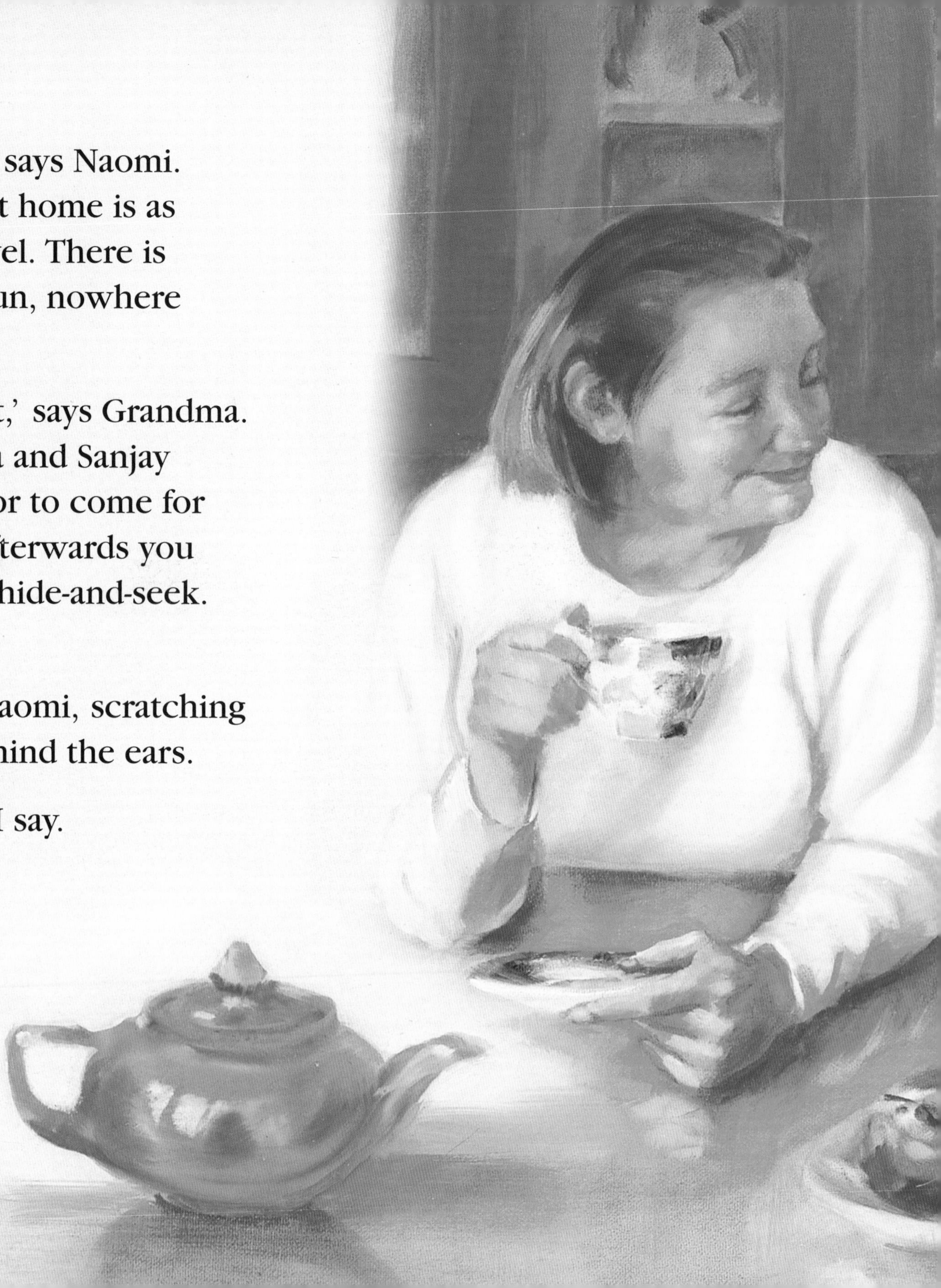

Big Cat jumps down and looks around. She stares steadily at Grandma, then she suddenly swivels around and starts chasing her tail. We all laugh and Grandma says, 'Big Cat! What are you up to? You're as frisky as a kitten.'

But Big Cat just keeps on chasing, chasing, chasing her tail, like a mad thing.

That night after dinner,
Sanjay, Asha, Naomi,
Small Dog and I spill out
of the house into the
deepest shadows.

As Naomi and I are creeping past the kitchen window, Big Cat jumps up onto the windowsill and miaows. Naomi and I glance up and as usual, there is Grandma, her hands in the sink.

Big Cat scratches at the windowpane. She miaows again. Louder. Grandma looks up. She smiles at Big Cat, and gives a little nod.

Then in two flicks of a dishcloth Grandma is out the door – streaking with us into the dark.

Naomi says, 'Grandma's excellent at hiding. Even Small Dog can't find her.'

Later that night, I bury my nose in Big Cat's fur and whisper, 'I'll tell you a secret. I saw Grandma scurry up that tree. Just like a little kid.'

Big Cat gives a rumbly miaow, as if she's saying, 'I know!' Then she yawns and shuts her eyes, and for a moment - just a moment - I am there with her, full of fizz and hiss, chasing after autumn leaves cartwheeling in the wind.

For Danny and Karen and our big cat, Lucy
M.W.

To my dearest daughter, Sunny, with love
A.S.

Original edition published by Penguin Books Australia Ltd.

Annick Press Ltd.

Canadian Cataloguing in Publication Data

Wild, Margaret, 1948-
Big cat dreaming

ISBN 1-55037-493-1

1. Picture books for children. I. Spudvilas, Anne.
II. Title.

PZ7.W645Bi 1997 j813'.54 C96-930024-7

The art in this book was rendered in oil.
The text was typeset in Garamond.

Distributed in Canada by:
Firefly Books Ltd.
3680 Victoria Park Avenue
Willowdale, ON M2H 3K1

Published in the U.S.A. by Annick Press (U.S.) Ltd.
Distributed in the U.S.A. by:
Firefly Books (U.S.) Inc.
P.O. Box 1338, Ellicott Station
Buffalo, NY 14205

Printed by Southbank Book.